Dieter Wiesmüller

Maury and the Nightpirates

The Overlook Press
WOODSTOCK, NEW YORK

Mann
12 Bedford St.
NYC 10014

The whole town was fast asleep. Only the light in Maury's room was still burning. He was angry because someone had taken his favorite book, the one with the red cover called *A Treasury of Great Pirate Tales*. He was looking out of his window, watching the moon play hide and seek with the clouds, when he heard a voice: "Ahoy Maury!" it called into the dark night air. It was coming from somewhere high up on the roof!

Maury grabbed his hat with the big blue feather, ran out of his room, around a few corners, up some steps, and was on the roof of his house in no time. Only Nero the black cat was allowed up here, but Maury didn't even notice him. What he saw was very strange: anchored to the chimney was a beautiful sailboat, floating lightly on the night-breeze. "Come aboard!" the voice was calling. "You must hurry, the night is short, and we have no time to lose!" Maury walked to the edge of the roof, climbed up the thirty-two steps of the rope ladder, and . . .

. . . found himself standing before resident ship
rat Victor Cabot, Pedro Balboa the disputatious
parrot, and Lissi Fillibuster, with her long black
hair and a single silver earring.
"Where are we going?" Maury asked.
"On a great adventure" Lissi said, smiling.
"Of all the terrible tempests!" Pedro croaked.
"Tonight we are going to get the treasure!"
Victor squeaked.
"Fantastic!" Maury cried, and jumped aboard.

They pulled up the anchor, and began sailing
through the sleeping town. Nero followed them
for a little while, running across the rooftops.
Suddenly Victor squealed. "Ahoy! Look ahead!
there's a big storm brewing in the distance".
"Oh no, not again!" Lissi said despairingly.
"Of all the miserable mast-breakers" cursed
Pedro. "And just when we're on the way to get
the treasure back!"
Maury hardly had time to ask "But what does
the storm have to do with the treasure?"
when . . .

. . . they were swallowed up in a thick black whirlwind of clouds and thrown from side to side. Lissi and Maury tried to control the rudder. Victor and Pedro held onto the ropes and each other, but no matter what they did, they could not keep the ship on course. Suddenly there was an even bigger gust of wind, and they were falling into the dark. Then an ear-splitting crash . . .

. . . and they had run aground! Maury was frightened, but Lissi, Victor and Pedro knew what to do. This was only the one-hundred-and-ninth time that they had to free their ship. "It's always the same," Pedro growled. "Every little storm sends us crashing to the ground."
Lissi threw a grappling hook over the railing, and everybody pulled as hard as they could. Finally they managed to free the ship.

Soon the sails were set, and they were floating through the trees. But which direction should they go? Would they ever get out of this dreadful forest? Without their friend Uri the owl, they would have been hopelessly lost. Flying ahead, she guided them safely out of the dark green labyrinth.

They had just risen above the trees, when Maury
asked impatiently: "How much further is it until
we get to the treasure?"
Lissi scanned the horizon through her telescope
and answered: "We must sail along the Silver
River and follow the moonlight across the sea.
When we get to an ancient, long-forgotten
lighthouse, that's where we'll find the treasure."
"That's all?" Maury grumbled. "That's not what I
call a real adventure."

"Of all the nitwitted nincompoops," Pedro thundered. "They won't give it up without a fight!"
"But who?" Maury cried.
"Pirate Scrimshaw and his notorious gang," Lissi whispered. "They have stolen many treasures."
"One hundred and nine times we asked Scrimshaw to give it back," Victor whistled from the crow's nest, "and one hundred and nine times he refused. So tonight, we're going to get it, no matter what."

"You can help us make a plan to outwit them," Lissi promised.
"But how?" Maury cried excitedly.
"Shhh . . . quiet. The lighthouse!"
Carefully they tied the ship alongside the tower and climbed over the railing. When Lissi opened a little round door, they found themselves in the spookiest, dreariest place imaginable. Lissi took Maury's hand, and the four of them tiptoed ahead into the impenetrable darkness. Round and round they went, down a never-ending spiral staircase, with hundreds and hundreds of steps . . .

. . . but suddenly, there was light! Of all the hair-raising hoodlums, it was the pirates. "Stop right there!" the biggest one growled with a dangerous glint in his eye. "Nobody gets past us!"
"That's what you think!" Lissi shouted, and dashed between his legs

. . . skipped down a few steps, and landed
right in the arms of Captain Scrimshaw!
"Of all the scurrilous skeletons," he roared,
"what are you doing in my treasure vault?"
"Oh Great Master of the Winds, I have a
gift for you!" Lissi said, pointing at Maury.
"Look, I have brought you a new cabin-boy!"
"This miserable milk-sop wants to be a
pirate?" Scrimshaw laughed.
Maury whispered "yes . . ."
"Of all the yellow-bellied buccaneers," the
old man thundered. "In that case, the first
thing we must teach him is the Pirate's
Alphabet and the Corsair's Code of Conduct."

Maury sat on a large barrel right next to Captain
Scrimshaw and got his first lesson.
"How do you tackle a luff?
When do you joggle a plank?
Where do you tie the futtock-hoop?
What is the cut of the Captain's jib?
This really wasn't what Maury thought pirate life
was like, but he pretended to find it terribly
interesting. Captain Scrimshaw kept on reading
aloud, page after page. This made him very
thirsty, and he drank one mug of rum after
another. But as everybody knows, too much rum
makes even the most ferocious pirate very sleepy.

The Captain fell forward with a mighty crash, fast asleep! Soon, the other pirates started snoring too. "Of all the pillaging plunderers, it worked!" Lissi whispered, dashing into the treasure vault. It didn't take long to find what they were looking for, and all Lissi said was "Take the red one and the blue one."

Without losing any time, they were on their way up the spiral staircase as fast as they could go.
"But what about the treasure?" Maury asked.
"Shh . . . quiet! Don't wake the pirates!" Lissi said.
The last thing the four friends heard before climbing back on board was an ear-splitting symphony of snores.

At last, Lissi, Victor, Pedro and Maury were safe.
"We did it! We got it back!" Lissi rejoiced.
"All this fuss, for some old books?" Maury asked.
"Yes!" Lissi shouted. "For me this is the greatest
treasure of them all, because it contains all the
secrets of sailing the ocean."
Lissi found the chapter "Sailing in Storms" just as
some menacing black clouds appeared on the
horizon. This time, with the help of their treasure,
the four friends continued to sail steadily on course
through the ferocious storm and soon had it safely
behind them.

The rest of their trip was quiet and peaceful. When they reached the outskirts of Maury's town, Lissi took the red book and handed it to Maury.

"It's an old time-honored tradition that at the end of each treasure-hunting trip, everyone gets their fair share. Here is yours!"

Maury climbed down to his roof and opened the book. It was *A Treasury of Great Pirate Tales,* his favorite book! Far away, Lissi called: "Ahoy Maury, Great Nightpirate!" Maury started to read, and soon he was very sleepy. That night he dreamt that a great ship came to take him away on a wonderful adventure . . .

First published in 1990 by
The Overlook Press
Lewis Hollow Road
Woodstock, New York 12498

Text and illustrations copyright © 1990 by
Dieter Wiesmüller
Translation copyright © 1990 by
The Overlook Press

Library of Congress Cataloging-in-Publication

Wiesmüller, Dieter.
    [Komm mit, Moritz.   English]
    Maury and the nightpirates / by Dieter
Wiesmüller.
        p.   cm.
    Translation of: Komm mit, Moritz.
    Summary: Maury goes for a night
  journey with some rather unusual pirates
  in a flying ship.
    [1. Pirates — Fiction.]   I. Title.
PZ7.W6366Mau   1990
[Fic]—dc20   89-77567   CIP   AC
ISBN 0-87951-392-6

Printed in Belgium